The Best Snowman

by Margaret Nash

Illustrated by Jörg Saupe

W

FRANKLIN WATTS
LONDON•SYDNEY

This editon 2009

Franklin Watts
338 Euston Road
London
NW1 3BH

Franklin Watts Australia
Level 17/207 Kent Street
Sydney
NSW 2000

A CIP catalogue record for this book is available
from the British Library.

ISBN 978 0 7496 9143 1

Series Editor: Louise John
Series Advisor: Dr Barrie Wade
Series Designer: Jason Anscomb

Printed in China

Franklin Watts is a division of
Hachette Children's Books,
an Hachette UK company.
www.hachette.co.uk

Ravi had never seen snow.
Then, one cold day, it came.

Ravi made a snowman as
fat as a barrel.

Then he stuck a saucepan
on its head.

"He's funny," said Mr Jones, who lived next door.

"Can you make one for me, too?"

"And me," said Mrs Cook

"And us," said Miss Ling
and Mr Parry.

"OK," said Ravi.

"I'll make snowmen for all of you."

"One like yours, please," said Mr Jones.

12

"As fat as a barrel!"

The snowman was a very funny shape.

But Mr Jones was pleased.

"A tall, thin one, please," said Miss Ling.

The snowman was so tall
and thin, it couldn't stand up.
But Miss Ling was pleased.

"I'd like a snow-woman, please," said Mrs Cook.

The hat was much too big

for the snow-woman.

But Mrs Cook was pleased.

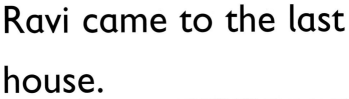

Ravi came to the last house.

20

"Oh, dear!" he said.

"A teeny-weeny snowman, please," said Mr Parry.

"They're the best."

So, Ravi made a snowman the size of a snowball.

"Why is he the best?" asked Ravi.

Mr Parry took the teeny-weeny snowman ...

and put him in the freezer
with the frozen peas.

"He's the best snowman because he won't melt," said Mr Parry.

And he didn't!

Puzzle 1

Put these pictures in the correct order.
Now tell the story in your own words.
How short can you make the story?

Puzzle 2

sad   curious

kind

pleased   delighted   eager   clever

unhappy   sorry

Choose the words which best describe
each character. Can you think of any
more? Pretend to be one of the characters!

Answers

Puzzle 1

The correct order is:

1d, 2e, 3a, 4f, 5c, 6b

Puzzle 2

Ravi: curious, kind

Mrs Cook: delighted, pleased

Mr Parry: clever, eager

Look out for more Leapfrog stories:

The Little Star
ISBN 978 0 7496 3833 7

Recycled!
ISBN 978 0 7496 4388 1

Jack's Party
ISBN 978 0 7496 4389 8

The Crying Princess
ISBN 978 0 7496 4632 5

Jasper and Jess
ISBN 978 0 7496 4081 1

The Lazy Scarecrow
ISBN 978 0 7496 4082 8

Big Bad Blob
ISBN 978 0 7496 7092 4*
ISBN 978 0 7496 7796 1

Cara's Breakfast
ISBN 978 0 7496 7093 1*
ISBN 978 0 7496 7797 8

Croc's Tooth
ISBN 978 0 7496 7799 2

The Magic Word
ISBN 978 0 7496 7096 2*
ISBN 978 0 7496 7800 5

Tim's Tent
ISBN 978 0 7496 7801 2

Why Not?
ISBN 978 0 7496 7094 8*
ISBN 978 0 7496 7798 5

Sticky Vickie
ISBN 978 0 7496 7986 6

Handyman Doug
ISBN 978 0 7496 7987 3

Billy and the Wizard
ISBN 978 0 7496 7985 9

Sam's Spots
ISBN 978 0 7496 7976 7*
ISBN 978 0 7496 7984 2

Bill's Baggy Trousers
ISBN 978 0 7496 3829 0

Bill's Bouncy Shoes
ISBN 978 0 7496 7990 3

Little Joe's Big Race
ISBN 978 0 7496 3832 0

Little Joe's Balloon Race
ISBN 978 0 7496 7989 7

Felix on the Move
ISBN 978 0 7496 4387 4

Felix and the Kitten
ISBN 978 0 7496 7988 0

The Cheeky Monkey
ISBN 978 0 7496 3830 6

Cheeky Monkey on Holiday
ISBN 978 0 7496 7991 0

For details of all our titles go to: www.franklinwatts.co.uk

*hardback